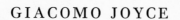

GIACOMO JOYCE

JAMES JOYCE

A photograph taken by Ottocaro Weiss in Zurich, 1915, soon after Joyce arrived there from Trieste.

GIACOMO JOYCE

BY JAMES JOYCE

With an Introduction and Notes by

RICHARD ELLMANN

New York / THE VIKING PRESS

First published in January 1968
as a limited edition by The Viking Press, Inc.
625 Madison Avenue, New York, N.Y. 10022

Reset and reissued in its present form May 1968

Library of Congress catalog card number: 67–28920

Printed in U.S.A.

Fragments of *Giacomo Joyce* are quoted in Richard Ellmann's *James
Joyce*, Oxford University Press (New York, 1959), and other excerpts in
Harper's Magazine, January 1968

CONTENTS

INTRODUCTION

It seems probable that *Giacomo Joyce* will be the last of James Joyce's published writings. He wrote it over half a century ago in Trieste, at that stage of his life when he was completing *A Portrait of the Artist as a Young Man* and was beginning *Ulysses*. *Giacomo Joyce* pivots between the two books. A love poem which is never recited, it is Joyce's attempt at the sentimental education of a dark lady, his farewell to a phase of his life, and at the same time his discovery of a new form of imaginative expression.

The manuscript was left by Joyce in Trieste and was saved from loss by his brother Stanislaus. It was subsequently acquired by a collector who prefers to remain anonymous. Joyce wrote it in his best calligraphic hand, without changes, on both sides of eight large sheets, which are loosely held within the nondescript blue-paper covers of a school notebook. The sheets are of heavy paper, oversize, of the sort ordinarily used for pencil sketches rather than for writing assignments. They are faintly reminiscent of those parchment sheets on which in 1909 Joyce wrote out the poems of *Chamber Music* for his wife. On the upper left-hand corner of the front cover, the name "Giacomo Joyce" is inscribed in another hand.

Giacomo Joyce

This Italian form of his name was never used by Joyce, and its acceptance here, to ornament a study of love, must have expressed his sense of *dépaysement* as a Triestine Dubliner pining for requital in two languages. He was content to keep what he had written under this heading, and it has seemed reasonable to follow his example, since the overtones of self-deflation suit the piece. Joyce allows no doubt that the hero is to be identified with himself, for he calls Giacomo "Jamesy" and "Jim," and once appeals to his wife as "Nora."

Giacomo Joyce displays its hero's erotic commotion over a girl pupil to whom he was teaching English. Joyce had many such pupils in Trieste, but he seems to associate his subject with one in particular, Amalia Popper, who lived on the via San Michele. Her father, Leopoldo Popper, may have furnished the first name for Bloom in *Ulysses*. But if he stood as model for the pupil's father, he was made to give up his imposing moustache and take on unaccustomed whiskers. Signorina Popper, afterwards the wife of Michele Risolo, died in 1967 in Florence. Her husband dates her lessons from Joyce in the years 1907 and 1908, and explains that, because she left Trieste to attend the universities of Vienna and Florence, she did not meet Joyce after 1909. If this recollection is accurate, then presumably Joyce either invented subsequent encounters or else transfused aspects of Signorina Popper into those of some successor among his pupils. The work makes clear, at any rate, that the incident—such as it was—ended before he left Trieste in 1915.

Joyce's prose writings are so committed to an Irish scene that among them *Giacomo Joyce* is distinct in being set on the continent. The city of Trieste, like Dublin, is presented obliquely, but, unlike Dublin, with only occasional place names. An upland road, a hospital, a piazza, a market appear deliberately unidentified. Yet they come into being as the girl or her family passes through them. The city is made recognizable with its up and down streets, the brown overlapping tiles of its roofs, the Cimitero Israelitico, the nationalistic chafing at Austro-Hungarian rule. Against it are counterposed images not only of Paris, as in *Ulysses*, but also of Padua and of the rice country near Vercelli. Through these continental scenes Giacomo moves, foreign and desirous, seabedabbled who once was fiery. As a character he is older and less arrogant than

Stephen, younger and more purposeful than Bloom, a middle son in their literary family.

The manuscript is not dated, but it describes a series of slender occurrences and swollen emotions that must have absorbed Joyce's mind over many months. It begins with the first class attended by his new pupil. Several events which are mentioned can be given a precise date. For example, at the Jewish cemetery Joyce is in the company of "pimply Meissel," who has come to mourn at his wife's grave. This was Filippo Meissel, whose wife, Ada Hirsch Meissel, committed suicide on October 20, 1911. Another indication of time is a reference to the expulsion of a music critic named Ettore Albini from La Scala in Milan, because he failed to stand when the "Marcia Reale," anthem of the Kingdom of Italy, was played. Albini, who wrote for the Roman socialist newspaper *Avanti!* rather than, as Joyce says, for the Turin daily *Il Secolo*, was expelled on December 17, 1911, at a benefit concert for the Italian Red Cross and the families of soldiers killed or wounded in Libya, where Italy was fighting the Turks.

Other references, out of sequence as often as in, indicate that more time has elapsed. A description of Padua at night must derive from Joyce's two trips to that city late in April 1912, when he went to be examined in the hope of qualifying to teach English at an Italian high school. The rice field near Vercelli which he remarks upon would be visible from the train between Milan and Turin; he took this route on his way to Ireland in July 1912. There is also an allusion to his lectures on *Hamlet* "to docile Trieste," when his audience included his pretty pupil. These lectures, expanded from the announced ten to twelve, took place from November 4, 1912, to February 10, 1913.

Some references to Joyce's books extend the composition of *Giacomo Joyce* to a still later date. He could scarcely have had a dream about *Ulysses* before 1914, the year that, as he always said afterward, the book first took shape in his mind. And he shows his pupil at least some of *A Portrait of the Artist as a Young Man*. Her comment that it was not frank for frankness' sake would be appropriate particularly if she had read the third chapter, where Stephen details and regrets his sins. This chapter had existed in manuscript form since 1908, but only in June 1914 did Joyce have it typed so that he could send it to the *Egoist* in London, where the novel was being serialized. At that time he evidently had other copies made, for he lent one to his friend Italo Svevo, and he indicates here that he lent another to his pupil. He was then still working on the last two of the book's five chapters. It would appear that the events and moods collocated in *Giacomo Joyce* took place between late 1911 and the middle of 1914. While Joyce probably relied to some extent on earlier notes, he could not have written it down as a whole before the end of June 1914.

He cannot have deferred it for long after that, because Chapter V of *A Portrait*, which he completed by November 11, 1914, contains from start to finish direct borrowings from *Giacomo Joyce*. Some are verbatim;

most are reworked, such as the passage, "My words in her mind: cold polished stones sinking through a quagmire," which becomes, in Chapter V, "The heavy lumpish phrase sank slowly out of hearing like a stone through a quagmire." Joyce was not the man to repeat himself, so it seems probable that at some time before mid-November of 1914 he had decided to pillage rather than to publish *Giacomo Joyce*. He did so not only for the sake of *A Portrait* but also for *Ulysses* and for his play *Exiles*.

The likeliest time, then, for the final version of *Giacomo Joyce* is July or August 1914. The impulsion to write it out may well have come from his friend Svevo, who in a letter to Joyce of June 26 commented on the newly published *Dubliners* and on the typescript of the first three chapters of *A Portrait*, and then asked, "When will you write an Italian work about our town? Why not?" Joyce liked to be prompted, and he had reason to pay particular attention to a prompting from Svevo, since Svevo's fictional method—of self-reduction followed by self-redemption through wit—was playing a part in the growing conception of Leopold Bloom. Moreover, Svevo's early novel *Senilità* (for which Joyce proposed the English title *As a Man Grows Older*) had opened up afresh the subject of the middle-aged man, actually only thirty-five, in love with a younger woman. No one had itemized and mocked the vexations that beset lovers of disparate ages with more shrewdness than Svevo. In this modern treatment of the

Nausicaa theme the hero, Emilio, combines his role as Angiolina's seducer with a more problematical one of being her moral instructor. He flounders in a sea of half-conscious intentions, not all of them bad, which Giacomo and Bloom (especially in his role as the philanderer "Henry Flower") could recognize. Joyce had a great admiration for Svevo's book, and particularly for its irony; in *Senilità* there were precursory intimations of his own theme, although Giacomo is a real rather than a self-styled teacher, and has an intentness, as his beloved has a style, which were inappropriate for Emilio and Angiolina.

In writing *Giacomo Joyce*, the fact that he had passed beyond thirty—portentous year—was similarly present to Joyce. He liked to remind his friends, a little pedantically, that the Romans had made seventeen the dividing line between *pueritia* and *adulescentia*, and thirty-one the beginning of *iuventus*. The sadness of being no longer an adolescent, even by Roman standards, so afflicted Joyce that in his thirty-first year he began to write poems again for the first time since *Chamber Music*. The first was "Watching the Needleboats at San Sabba," in which he drew upon Puccini's *La Fanciulla del West* for his refrain:

> I heard their young hearts crying
> Loveward above the glancing oar
> And heard the prairie grasses sighing:
> *No more, return no more!*

O hearts, O sighing grasses,
Vainly your loveblown bannerets mourn!
No more will the wild wind that passes
Return, no more return.

This poem, written in September 1913, was followed by
"A Flower Given to My Daughter," a gift he acknowl-
edges also in *Giacomo Joyce*, and by *"Tutto è sciolto"*
(July 13, 1914), and "Nightpiece" (1915), both closely
connected with the same love affair, as well as by other
poems more tenuously connected with it. All pursue,
in the rather anemic style he reserved for his verse, that
theme which in *Giacomo Joyce* he associates with
Sweelinck's variations for the clavichord on "Youth
Has an End":

> *Mein junges Leben hat ein End,*
> *Mein Freud und auch mein Leid,*
> *Mein arme Seele soll behend*
> *Scheiden von meinem Leib.*
> *Mein Leben kann nicht länger stehn,*
> *Es ist sehr schwach und muss vergehn*
> *In Todeskampf und Streit.**

Such painful misgivings are presented in *Giacomo
Joyce* through a series of at once lush and sterile encounters. These take place at different spatial levels,
always confirming distance. The pupil is conspicu-

---

* "My youth has an end, my joy and sorrow too, my poor soul will quickly
part from my body. My life can no longer stand firm, it is very feeble and
must perish in death agony and struggle."

ously higher, "a young woman of quality" in her comfortable house up the hilly via San Michele. Wrapped in odorous furs, herself strangely odorless, she stares through a lorgnette, tapping high heels, while he is below, eyeing "upward from night and mud." Once, at the opera, he sits above her, but there his position is even more inferior, for he is in the top gallery, surrounded by the plebeians and their smells, and, himself unseen, gazes down at her cool small beauty, her green-dressed body and pinnacled hair below among the expensive people.

In the course of these shifting perspectives, Joyce unfolds the paradigm of unsatisfied love as it takes hold of the no longer young. Giacomo, whose diffidence if treated with less irony would be humid, records the different inflections of his desire; he admires and sympathizes with his pupil, patronizes and secretly mocks her, hints, holds back, fails to speak out, succumbs like Stephen and Bloom to morose delectation—diet of writers—and phrases with searing expertness his ludicrous unsuccess. The language shifts at moments to Shakespeare's diction, applied not only to love's tenderness but to "pox-fouled wenches," and evokes with that diction an atmosphere of castles, princely hesitation, blazonry, court proprieties, Polonius with his daughter; but then it quickly diverges to two manners of Joyce's own, the coiling of words upon themselves in enwound repetition, to follow the "curve of an emotion," as in much of *A Portrait*, and the newer manner he was evolving for *Ulysses*, of sharp, certain, shorthand phrases which need no signaled emphasis.

From the beginning, when the pupil emerges out of nowhere to make him question, "Who?", she is remote, pale, impalpable, removed from him by her glasses, by never blowing her nose, by her cobweb handwriting, by her Jewishness, by her sheltered rearing, by her natural distinction, by her unaccountable and insurmountable virtue. Often the scene is misted, cloudy, vaporous, surrounded by ghosts at various degrees of manifestation, as if to envelop in an ominous and even deadly uncertainty both her and his passion for her. In *Finnegans Wake* Joyce makes another daughter, Anna Livia's, into a cloud, and some association of nubile and nubilous seems here to be coming into his head.

And yet, among the clouds, he does not fail to summon up with sinuous precision his pupil's distinctive being, her disconcerted recoils from his timid onslaughts, her fatigued delicacy, her intellectual ambition, her unceasing desirability. In the last pages the situation becomes hallucinatory; dream images thicken. He has fathomed her essence so completely that their eyes (like Donne's twisting eyebeams) have intermingled. For a moment, like Robert Hand in *Exiles*, he dreams that she has been his. "In sleep a king, but waking no such matter." What wakens him is her queenly verdict, from which a single phrase is quoted: "Because otherwise I could not see you." This rebuff is no more acceptable for having been anticipated. Yet the field is not altogether lost: "What then? Write it, damn you, write it! What else are you good for?" If he is not Prince Hamlet any more than he is Christ (though both parallels spring to his mind), he has at least something in common with Shakespeare. "Assumed dongiovannism will not save him," as Stephen says of his equally deprived and inept Shakespeare in *Ulysses*. Like all Joyce's books, *Giacomo Joyce* wryly grants the power of love even as it attests the melancholy of human attempts to enjoy it.

In the final act of writing, the appearance of the work on the page may have become an element of its substance. Perhaps with Mallarmé in mind, Joyce joined and disjoined the entries by pauses of varying duration measured by spaces of varying length. Different intensities of silence seem mustered to alternate with clusters of laconic or undulatory speech. On the next to last page, for example, the clotted images are reinforced by dense handwriting and the absence of pause.

After Joyce had brought himself to copying *Giacomo Joyce*, he had next to bring himself to not publishing it. Since it was so expatriated, so open about his frailties, so little impersonalized (even if ironically detached) as to play truant from the aesthetic school just opened by Stephen Dedalus, Joyce was perhaps the readier to consider its abandonment. He had the precedent of his epiphanies, written more than ten years before with the kindred aim of exposing "the motions of my spirit," and ultimately relegated to form pages of *Stephen Hero*. Yet he evidently liked *Giacomo Joyce* too much in itself to sacrifice it, whatever later frugalities he might practice, before he had stamped his approval by making a fair copy.

The spirit of *Giacomo Joyce* was now diffused. Its heroine, whom Giacomo relates to Beatrice Portinari and Beatrice Cenci, is related also to Beatrice Justice in *Exiles*. This Beatrice has similarly weak eyes—surrounded by beautiful lashes—with which she too has read the hero's earlier writings. In the play's first act she explains why she has come to Richard's house, and the words she uses are almost the same as the only words spoken directly by Giacomo's pupil: "Otherwise I could not see you." The remark, which devastates Giacomo, is reset in a context where it flatters Richard, indicating what Joyce elsewhere called the power of liberating oneself through art. Defeat in Trieste can transcribe as victory in Dublin.

Feelings registered in *Giacomo Joyce* proved applicable also to *A Portrait of the Artist as a Young Man*. The new erotic emotions served to refurbish those of ten years before, now attenuated. That Stephen's girl was supposed to be symbolic of the Irish race, as Giacomo's is of the Jewish race, offered little impediment; in *Ulysses* Joyce would demonstrate with all possible dexterity the interchangeability of the two races. Both girls are dark and virginal, though both (like Bertha in *Exiles*) have to submit to imaginary possession by their

admirers' minds. In keeping with the sensory prefer-
ences of *A Portrait*, the Irish girl is accorded "a wild
and languid smell," which is denied her Triestine sister.

Then Stephen, pondering a line from Thomas Nash,
calls before his mind the age of Elizabeth:

> Eyes, opening from the darkness of desire, eyes that
> dimmed the breaking east. What was their languid grace
> but the softness of chambering? And what was their
> shimmer but the shimmer of the scum that mantled the
> cesspool of the court of a slobbering Stuart. And he tasted
> in the language of memory ambered wines, dying fallings
> of sweet airs, the proud pavan: and saw with the eyes of
> memory kind gentlewomen in Covent Garden wooing
> from their balconies with sucking mouths and the pox-
> fouled wenches of the taverns and young wives that, gaily
> yielding to their ravishers, clipped and clipped again.
>
> The images he had summoned gave him no pleasure.
> They were secret and enflaming but her image was not
> entangled by them. That was not the way to think of her.
> It was not even the way in which he thought of her. Could
> his mind then not trust itself? Old phrases, sweet only
> with a disinterred sweetness like the figseeds Cranly rooted
> out of his gleaming teeth.

The first paragraph is only a little altered from
Giacomo Joyce; the second repudiates the first, as do
later sentences. Giacomo does not accomplish so explicit
a repudiation; he need not debate his vocabularies, he
merely shifts them as moods shift. In *Ulysses* Joyce
follows Giacomo's rather than Stephen's method. The

clashing of dictions like rival assaults becomes, in fact, the device to replace, in Joyce's later work, the elaborate and faintly precious interweavings of colored words. In the same way, the erratic, contorted introspection of *Giacomo Joyce* helps to deflect *A Portrait* from third-person narrative to Stephen's first-person diary at the end of that book, and prepares for the interior monologues of Bloom and Stephen.

As he came to *Ulysses*, Joyce took sentences from *Giacomo Joyce* and made them into whole paragraphs or longer units. Some slipped easily from work to work: morning in Trieste became morning in Paris, to be observed by Stephen more rancorously than was its correlative by Giacomo. A twilight image of mother and daughter, as a mare and her fillyfoal, is made entirely and beautifully equine for the *Oxen of the Sun* episode. The confrontation of Irishman and Jew is primarily a matter of male friendship rather than of heterosexual amorousness, and instead of lamenting the ageing process with Giacomo, Joyce apportions middle age to Bloom and youth to Stephen. Some of the scenes—the classroom, the graveyard, the Paduan brothels—are imported from the Adriatic to the Liffey; a carriage ride of the pupil's family through a crowded market is exalted into a viceregal cavalcade; a blind man ceases to beg and tunes pianos instead. Oliver St. John Gogarty, eternal antagonist, who makes a brief dream-visit to Giacomo in Trieste, turns up again in Dublin as Mulligan. The fits and starts with which Giacomo's passion mounts are cognate with the discontinuous episodes and perspectives in *Ulysses*. Both books move, too, toward Circean images of the unconscious, where the double sense of misbehavior and compunction reaches a phantasmagoric climax marked by satanic metaphor.

Much later in the composition of *Ulysses*, at the end of 1918, Joyce approached a brunette on a Zurich street and expressed his astonishment at her resemblance to a girl he had seen in Dublin. In his subsequent correspondence with this Martha Fleischmann, he attached extraordinary consequence to the possibility that she might be Jewish. Apparently he was looking for a new, and of necessity Swiss, embodiment of that Judaeo-Celtic composite he had loved in Trieste. Martha Fleischmann in turn became a model for Gerty Mac-Dowell in the *Nausicaa* episode, which parodies the possession by long distance about which Giacomo had bragged in Trieste, and Stephen brooded in Dublin. On a shabby genteel level, Bloom attempts psychic seduction of Martha Clifford as well, by writing letters to her, and so mimics ironically Joyce's own use of a literary medium to achieve a similar occult goal.

A good deal of Joyce's writing can be seen to allude, at least *sotto voce*, to his middle-aged romance. Yet he infuses *Giacomo Joyce* also with independent life, and it stands now in its own terms as a great achievement. To readers accustomed by Joyce to large formal structures, the size and informality of this most delicate of novels may be especially ingratiating. When, not long before his death, Joyce said he would write something very simple and very short, he was thinking perhaps of how he had solidified the small, fragile, transitory perfection of his Triestine pupil into the small, fragile, enduring perfection of *Giacomo Joyce*.

RICHARD ELLMANN

THE TEXT OF THE NOTEBOOK

A page-for-page transcription in type

Numbers in brackets indicate the pages of the notebook. Except for 15, the text corresponds page for page to the original.

Who? A pale face surrounded by heavy odorous furs. Her movements are shy and nervous. She uses quizzing-glasses.

Yes: a brief syllable. A brief laugh. A brief beat of the eyelids.

Cobweb handwriting, traced long and fine with quiet disdain and resignation: a young person of quality.

I launch forth on an easy wave of tepid speech: Swedenborg, the pseudo-Areopagite, Miguel de Molinos, Joachim Abbas. The wave is spent. Her classmate, re-twisting her twisted body, purrs in boneless Viennese Italian: *Che coltura!* The long eyelids beat and lift: a burning needleprick stings and quivers in the velvet iris.

High heels clack hollow on the resonant stone stairs. Wintry air in the castle, gibbeted coats of mail, rude iron sconces over the windings of the winding turret stairs. Tapping clacking heels, a high and hollow noise. There is one below would speak with your ladyship.

[*1*]

She never blows her nose. A form of speech: the lesser for the greater.

Rounded and ripened: rounded by the lathe of inter-marriage and ripened in the forcing-house of the seclusion of her race.

A ricefield near Vercelli under creamy summer haze. The wings of her drooping hat shadow her false smile. Shadows streak her falsely smiling face, smitten by the hot creamy light, grey wheyhued shadows under the jawbones, streaks of eggyolk yellow on the moistened brow, rancid yellow humour lurking within the softened pulp of the eyes.

A flower given by her to my daughter. Frail gift, frail giver, frail blue-veined child.

Padua far beyond the sea. The silent middle age, night, darkness of history sleep in the *Piazza delle Erbe* under the moon. The city sleeps. Under the arches in the dark streets near the river the whores' eyes spy out for fornicators. *Cinque servizi per cinque franchi.* A dark wave of sense, again and again and again.
    Mine eyes fail in darkness, mine eyes fail,
    Mine eyes fail in darkness, love.
Again. No more. Dark love, dark longing. No more. Darkness.

Twilight. Crossing the *piazza*. Grey eve lowering on wide sagegreen pasturelands, shedding silently dusk and dew. She follows her mother with ungainly grace, the mare leading her filly foal. Grey twilight moulds softly the slim and shapely haunches, the meek supple tendonous neck, the fine-boned skull. Eve, peace, the dusk of wonder . . . . Hillo! Ostler! Hilloho!

[3]

Papa and the girls sliding downhill, astride of a to-
boggan: the Grand Turk and his harem. Tightly capped
and jacketted, boots laced in deft crisscross over the
flesh-warmed tongue, the short skirt taut from the round
knobs of the knees. A white flash: a flake, a snowflake:
And when she next doth ride abroad
May I be there to see!

I rush out of the tobacco-shop and call her name. She
turns and halts to hear my jumbled words of lessons,
hours, lessons, hours: and slowly her pale cheeks are
flushed with a kindling opal light. Nay, nay, be not
afraid!

Mio padre: she does the simplest acts with distinction. *Unde derivatur? Mia figlia ha una grandissima ammirazione per il suo maestro inglese.* The old man's face, handsome, flushed, with strongly Jewish features and long white whiskers, turns towards me as we walk down the hill together. O! Perfectly said: courtesy, benevolence, curiosity, trust, suspicion, naturalness, helplessness of age, confidence, frankness, urbanity, sincerity, warning, pathos, compassion: a perfect blend. Ignatius Loyola, make haste to help me!

This heart is sore and sad. Crossed in love?

Long lewdly leering lips: dark-blooded molluscs

Moving mists on the hill as I look upward from night and mud. Hanging mists over the damp trees. A light in the upper room. She is dressing to go to the play. There are ghosts in the mirror . . . . . Candles! Candles!

A gentle creature. At midnight, after music, all the way up the via San Michele, these words were spoken softly. Easy now, Jamesy! Did you never walk the streets of Dublin at night sobbing another name?

Corpses of Jews lie about me rotting in the mould of their holy field. Here is the tomb of her people, black stone, silence without hope . . . . . Pimply Meissel brought me here. He is beyond those trees standing with covered head at the grave of his suicide wife, wondering how the woman who slept in his bed has come to this end . . . . . The tomb of her people and hers: black stone, silence without hope: and all is ready. Do not die!

She raises her arms in an effort to hook at the nape of her neck a gown of black veiling. She cannot: no, she cannot. She moves backwards towards me mutely. I raise my arms to help her: her arms fall. I hold the websoft edges of her gown and drawing them out to hook them I see through the opening of the black veil her lithe body sheathed in an orange shift. It slips its ribbons of moorings at her shoulders and falls slowly: a lithe smooth naked body shimmering with silvery scales. It slips slowly over the slender buttocks of smooth polished silver and over their furrow, a tarnished silver shadow . . . . Fingers, cold and calm and moving . . . . A touch, a touch.

Small witless helpless and thin breath. But bend and hear: a voice. A sparrow under the wheels of Juggernaut, shaking shaker of the earth. Please, mister God, big mister God! Goodbye, big world! . . . . *Aber das ist eine Schweinerei!*

Great bows on her slim bronze shoes: spurs of a pampered fowl.

The lady goes apace, apace, apace . . . . . Pure air on the upland road. Trieste is waking rawly: raw sunlight over its huddled browntiled roofs, testudoform; a multitude of prostrate bugs await a national deliverance. Belluomo rises from the bed of his wife's lover's wife: the busy housewife is astir, sloe-eyed, a saucer of acetic acid in her hand . . . . . Pure air and silence on the upland road: and hoofs. A girl on horseback. Hedda! Hedda Gabler!

The sellers offer on their altars the first fruits: greenflecked lemons, jewelled cherries, shameful peaches with torn leaves. The carriage passes through the lane of canvas stalls, its wheel-spokes spinning in the glare. Make way! Her father and his son sit in the carriage. They have owls' eyes and owls' wisdom. Owlish wisdom stares from their eyes brooding upon the lore of their *Summa contra Gentiles*.

She thinks the Italian gentlemen were right to haul Ettore Albini, the critic of the *Secolo*, from the stalls because he did not stand up when the band played the Royal March. She heard that at supper. Ay. They love their country when they are quite sure which country it is.

She listens: virgin most prudent.

A skirt caught back by her sudden moving knee; a white lace edging of an underskirt lifted unduly; a leg-stretched web of stocking. *Si pol?*

I play lightly, softly singing, John Dowland's languid song. *Loth to depart:* I too am loth to go. That age is here and now. Here, opening from the darkness of desire, are eyes that dim the breaking East, their shimmer the shimmer of the scum that mantles the cesspool of the court of slobbering James. Here are wines all ambered, dying fallings of sweet airs, the proud pavan, kind gentlewomen wooing from their balconies with sucking mouths, the pox-fouled wenches and young wives that, gaily yielding to their ravishers, clip and clip again.

In the raw veiled spring morning faint odours float of morning Paris: aniseed, damp sawdust, hot dough of bread: and as I cross the Pont Saint Michel the steel-blue waking waters chill my heart. They creep and lap about the island whereon men have lived since the stone age . . . . . Tawny gloom in the vast gargoyled church. It is cold as on that morning: *quia frigus erat.* Upon the steps of the far high altar, naked as the body of the Lord, the ministers lie prostrate in weak prayer. The voice of an unseen reader rises, intoning the lesson from Hosea. *Haec dicit Dominus: in tribulatione sua mane consurgent ad me. Venite et revertamur ad Dominum* . . . . She stands beside me, pale and chill, clothed with the shadows of the sindark nave, her thin elbow at my arm. Her flesh recalls the thrill of that raw mist-veiled morning, hurrying torches, cruel eyes. Her soul is sorrowful, trembles and would weep. Weep not for me, O daughter of Jerusalem!

I expound Shakespeare to docile Trieste: Hamlet, quoth I, who is most courteous to gentle and simple is rude only to Polonius. Perhaps, an embittered idealist, he can see in the parents of his beloved only grotesque attempts on the part of nature to produce her image . . . . Marked you that?

She walks before me along the corridor and as she walks a dark coil of her hair slowly uncoils and falls. Slowly uncoiling, falling hair. She does not know and walks before me, simple and proud. So did she walk by Dante in simple pride and so, stainless of blood and violation, the daughter of Cenci, Beatrice, to her death:

> . . . . *Tie*
> *My girdle for me and bind up this hair*
> *In any simple knot.*

The housemaid tells me that they had to take her away at once to the hospital, *poveretta*, that she suffered so much, so much, *poveretta*, that it is very grave . . . . . . I walk away from her empty house. I feel that I am about to cry. Ah, no! It will not be like that, in a moment, without a word, without a look. No, no! Surely hell's luck will not fail me!

Operated. The surgeon's knife has probed in her entrails and withdrawn, leaving the raw jagged gash of its passage on her belly. I see her full dark suffering eyes, beautiful as the eyes of an antelope. O cruel wound! Libidinous God!

Once more in her chair by the window, happy words on her tongue, happy laughter. A bird twittering after storm, happy that its little foolish life has fluttered out of reach of the clutching fingers of an epileptic lord and giver of life, twittering happily, twittering and chirping happily.

She says that, had *The Portrait of the Artist* been frank only for frankness' sake, she would have asked why I had given it to her to read. O you would, would you? A lady of letters.

She stands black-robed at the telephone. Little timid laughs, little cries, timid runs of speech suddenly broken . . . . *Parlerò colla mamma* . . . . Come! chook, chook! come! The black pullet is frightened: little runs suddenly broken, little timid cries: it is crying for its mamma, the portly hen.

Loggione. The sodden walls ooze a steamy damp. A symphony of smells fuses the mass of huddled human forms: sour reek of armpits, nozzled oranges, melting breast ointments, mastick water, the breath of suppers of sulphurous garlic, foul phosphorescent farts, opoponax, the frank sweat of marriageable and married womankind, the soapy stink of men . . . . . . All night I have watched her, all night I shall see her: braided and pinnacled hair and olive oval face and calm soft eyes. A green fillet upon her hair and about her body a green-broidered gown: the hue of the illusion of the vegetable glass of nature and of lush grass, the hair of graves.

My words in her mind: cold polished stones sinking through a quagmire.

Those quiet cold fingers have touched the pages, foul and fair, on which my shame shall glow for ever. Quiet and cold and pure fingers. Have they never erred?

Her body has no smell: an odourless flower.

On the stairs. A cold frail hand: shyness, silence: dark langour-flooded eyes: weariness.

Whirling wreaths of grey vapour upon the heath. Her face, how grey and grave! Dank matted hair. Her lips press softly, her sighing breath comes through. Kissed.

My voice, dying in the echoes of its words, dies like the wisdom-wearied voice of the Eternal calling on Abraham through echoing hills. She leans back against the pillowed wall: odalisque-featured in the luxurious obscurity. Her eyes have drunk my thoughts: and into the moist warm yielding welcoming darkness of her womanhood my soul, itself dissolving, has streamed and poured and flooded a liquid and abundant seed . . . . . . Take her now who will! . . . .

[*14*]

As I come out of Ralli's house I come upon her suddenly as we both are giving alms to a blind beggar. She answers my sudden greeting by turning and averting her black basilisk eyes. *E col suo vedere attosca l'uomo quando lo vede.* I thank you for the word, messer Brunetto.

They spread under my feet carpets for the son of man. They await my passing. She stands in the yellow shadow of the hall, a plaid cloak shielding from chills her sinking shoulders: and as I halt in wonder and look about me she greets me wintrily and passes up the staircase darting at me for an instant out of her sluggish sidelong eyes a jet of liquorish venom.

A soft crumpled peagreen cover drapes the lounge. A narrow Parisian room. The hairdresser lay here but now. I kissed her stocking and the hem of her rustblack dusty skirt. It is the other. She. Gogarty came yesterday to be introduced. *Ulysses* is the reason. Symbol of the intellectual conscience . . . . Ireland then? And the husband? Pacing the corridor in list shoes or playing chess against himself. Why are we left here? The hairdresser lay here but now, clutching my head between her knobby knees . . . . Intellectual symbol of my race. Listen! The plunging gloom has fallen. Listen!
—I am not convinced that such activities of the mind or body can be called unhealthy—
She speaks. A weak voice from beyond the cold stars. Voice of wisdom. Say on! O, say again, making me wise! This voice I never heard.
She coils towards me along the crumpled lounge. I cannot move or speak. Coiling approach of starborn flesh. Adultery of wisdom. No. I will go. I will.
—Jim, love!—
Soft sucking lips kiss my left armpit: a coiling kiss on myriad veins. I burn! I crumple like a burning leaf! From my right armpit a fang of flame leaps out. A starry snake has kissed me: a cold nightsnake. I am lost!
—Nora!—

[15]

Jan Pieters Sweelink. The quaint name of the old Dutch musician makes all beauty seem quaint and far. I hear his variations for the clavichord on an old air: *Youth has an end*. In the vague mist of old sounds a faint point of light appears: the speech of the soul is about to be heard. Youth has an end: the end is here. It will never be. You know that well. What then? Write it, damn you, write it! What else are you good for?

"Why?"
"Because otherwise I could not see you."
Sliding—space—ages—foliage of stars—and waning heaven—stillness—and stillness deeper—stillness of annihilation—and her voice.

Non hunc sed Barabbam!

Unreadiness. A bare apartment. Torbid daylight. A long black piano: coffin of music. Poised on its edge a woman's hat, red-flowered, and umbrella, furled. Her arms: a casque, gules, and blunt spear on a field, sable.

Envoy: Love me, love my umbrella.

GIACOMO JOYCE

Facsimile pages

The following are facsimiles of pages 1, 11, 15, and 16, reduced photographically by about one-half.

Who? A pale face surrounded by heavy odorous furs. His movements are shy and nervous. She uses quizzing-glasses.

Yes: a brief syllable. A brief laugh. A brief beat of the eyelids.

Cobweb handwriting, traced long and fine with quiet disdain and resignation: a young person of quality.

I launch forth on an easy wave of tepid speech: Swedenborg, the pseudo-Areopagite, Miguel de Molinos, Joachim Abbas. The wave is spent. Her classmate, retwisting her twisted body, purrs in boneless Viennese Italian: Che coltura! The long eyelids beat and lift: a burning needleprick stings and quivers in the velvet iris.

High heels clack hollow on the resonant stone stairs. Wintry air in the castle, gibbeted coats of mail, rude iron sconces over the windings of the winding turret stairs. Tapping clacking heels, a high and hollow noise. There is one below would speak with your ladyship.

She walks before me along the corridor and as she walks a dark coil of her hair slowly uncoils and falls. Slowly uncoiling, falling hair! She does not know and walks before me, simple and proud. So did she walk by Dante in simple pride and so, stainless of blood and violation, the daughter of Cenci, Beatrice, to her death:

My girdle for me and tie up this hair *Tie*
In any simple knot.

The housemaid tells me that they had to take her away at once to the hospital, poveretta! that she suffered so much, so much, poveretta, that it is very grave...... I walk away from her empty house. I feel that I am about to cry. Ah, no! It will not be like that, in a moment, without a word, without a look. No, no! Surely hell's luck will not fail me!

Operated. The surgeon's knife has probed in her entrails and withdrawn, leaving the raw jagged gash of its passage on her belly. I see her full dark suffering eyes, beautiful as the eyes of an antelope. O cruel wound! Libidinous God!

Once more in her chair by the window, happy words on her tongue, happy laughter. A bird twittering after storm, happy that its little foolish life has fluttered out of reach of the clutching fingers of an epileptic lord and giver of life, twittering happily, twittering and chirping happily.

As I come out of Ralli's house I come upon her suddenly as we both are giving alms to a blind beggar. She answers my sudden greeting by turning and averting her black basilisk eyes. _E col suo vedere attosca l'uomo quando lo vede._ I thank you for the word, messer Brunetto.

They spread under my feet carpets for the son of man. They await my passing. She stands in the yellow shadow of the hall, a plaid cloak shielding from chills her sinking shoulders: and as I halt in wonder and look about me she greets me wintrily and passes up the staircase darting at me for an instant out of her sluggish sidelong eyes a jet of liquorish venom.

A soft crumpled peagreen cover drapes the lounge. A narrow Parisian room. The hairdresser lay here but now. I kissed her stocking and the hem of her rustblack dusty skirt. It is the other. She. Gogarty came yesterday to be introduced. _Ulysses_ is the reason. Symbol of the intellectual conscience .... Ireland then? And the husband? Pacing the corridor in list shoes or playing chess against himself. Why are we left here? The hairdresser lay here but now, clutching my head between her knobby knees .... Intellectual symbol of my race. Listen! The plunging gloom has fallen. Listen!
— I am not convinced that such activities of the mind or body can be called unhealthy —
She speaks. A weak voice from beyond the cold stars. Voice of wisdom. Say on! O, say again, making me wise! This voice I never heard.
She coils towards me along the crumpled lounge. I cannot move or speak. Coiling approach of starborn flesh. Adultery of wisdom. No. I will go. I will.
— Jim, love! —
Soft sucking lips kiss my left armpit: a coiling kiss on myriad veins. I burn! I crumple like a burning leaf! From my right armpit a fang of flame leaps out. A starry snake has kissed me: a cold nightsnake. I am lost!
— Nora! —

Jan Pieters Sweelink. The quaint name of the old Dutch musician makes all beauty seem quaint and far. I hear his variations for the clavichord on an old air : Youth has an end. In the vague mist of old sounds a faint point of light appears : the speech of the soul is about to be heard. Youth has an end : the end is here. It will never be. You know that well. What then ? Write it, damn you, write it ! What else are you good for ?

"Why?"
"Because otherwise I could not see you."
Sliding — space — ages — foliage of stars — and waning heaven — stillness — and stillness deeper — stillness of annihilation — and her voice.

<u>Non hunc sed Barabbam !</u>

Unreadiness. A bare apartment. Torrid daylight. A long black piano : coffin of music. Poised on its side a woman's hat, red-flowered, and umbrella, furled. Her arms : a casque, gules, and blunt spear on a field, sable.

Envoy : Love me, love my umbrella.

NOTES

Quotations from Joyce's works are cited from the following editions: *A Portrait of the Artist as a Young Man* (New York, The Viking Press, 1964, and London, Jonathan Cape, 1960); *Ulysses* (New York, Random House, 1961, and London, The Bodley Head, 1960); *Exiles* (New York, The Viking Press, 1951, and London, Jonathan Cape, 1936).

Page numbers are given first for the American edition and then in parenthesis for the English.

Page Paragraph

1   1   *furs . . . quizzing-glasses:* Conspicuously worn also by Mrs. Bellingham in *Ulysses*, pp. 465–66 (591), 468 (594).

      3   *Swedenborg, the pseudo-Areopagite, Miguel de Molinos:* discussed at some length in *The Critical Writings of James Joyce* (The Viking Press and Faber & Faber, 1959), especially pp. 134, 220–22.

            Joachim Abbas: quoted by Stephen in *Ulysses*, pp. 39–40 (49), at the point of the manuscript Joyce had completed just before leaving Trieste for Zurich in 1915.

2   2   *seclusion of her race:* Stephen similarly insists that his Irish girl possesses "the secret of her race" in *A Portrait,* p. 221 (225).

          3   *softened pulp:* "Mawkish pulp . . . Soft, warm . . ." *Ulysses,* p. 176 (224).

3   1   *A flower . . . blue-veined child:* Joyce wrote of the same incident in "A Flower Given to My Daughter," a poem dated "Trieste, 1913." A "frail pallor" is also characteristic of Stephen's girl in *A Portrait,* pp. 222–23 (227).

          3   *Twilight . . . the fine-boned skull:* Joyce probably consulted *Giacomo Joyce* again on his return to Trieste from Zurich in 1919, when he was working on the *Oxen of the Sun* episode. The result was a passage in *Ulysses,* p. 414 (541–42):

"The voices blend and fuse in clouded silence: silence that is the infinite of space: and swiftly, silently the soul is wafted over regions of cycles of cycles of generations that have lived. A region where grey twilight ever descends, never falls on wide sagegreen pasturefields, shedding her dusk, scattering a perennial dew of stars. She follows her mother with ungainly steps, a mare leading her fillyfoal. Twilight phantoms are they yet moulded in prophetic grace of structure, slim shapely haunches, a supple tendonous neck, the meek apprehensive skull. They fade, sad phantoms: all is gone. Agendath is a waste land, a home of screechowls and the sandblind upupa. Netaim, the golden, is no more. And on the highway of the clouds they come, muttering thunder of rebellion, the ghosts of beasts. Huuh! Hark! Huuh!"

The fillyfoal, "equine portent," gradually turns into Millicent Bloom.

          3   *Hillo! Ostler! Hilloho!* Stephen, also under

Shakespeare's influence, cries out "Hola! Hillyho!" *Ulysses*, p. 572 (674).

4   1   *boots laced in deft crisscross:* "to lace up crisscrossed" is part of Bloom's punishment. *Ulysses*, p. 529 (643).

And when she . . . there to see: Slightly modified from William Cowper, "John Gilpin."

5   1   *Ignatius Loyola, make haste to help me!* Stephen invokes the same aid for his theory of Shakespeare. *Ulysses*, p. 188 (241).

7   1   *A touch, a touch:* Molly says, "Give us a touch, Poldy." *Ulysses*, p. 89 (110).

8   2   *Trieste is waking . . . in her hand:* Transferred to Ulysses, p. 42 (52-53), this became:

"Paris rawly waking, crude sunlight on her lemon streets. Moist pith of farls of bread, the frog-green wormwood, her matin incense, court the air. Belluomo rises from the bed of his wife's lover's wife, the kerchiefed housewife is astir, a saucer of acetic acid in her hands. In Rodot's Yvonne and Madeleine newmake their tumbled beauties, shattering with gold teeth *chaussons* of pastry, their mouths yellowed with the *pus* of *flan breton*. Faces of Paris men go by, their wellpleased pleasers, curled conquistadores."

Pure air and silence on the upland road: and hoofs: Cf. "the sound of hoofs upon the road." *A Portrait*, p. 251 (255).

3   *shameful peaches:* Boylan's fruit purchase consists of "ripe shamefaced peaches," *Ulysses*, p. 227 (291).

9   1   *Ettore Albini:* Albini (1869–1954) was repeatedly jailed or deported for his indomitable opposition to the monarchy, to fascism, and to nationalism. For other details see Introduction.

9 1 *They love . . . country it is:* The same remark is attributed to J. J. O'Molloy in *Ulysses*, p. 337 (438).

    3 *Si pol:* In good Triestine, *"Se pol?"* and in Italian, *"Si può?"* ("Is it permitted?" "May I?") The expression, suitable for a servant asking to enter a room, is used by the buffoon Tonio as he begins his Prologue to Leoncavallo's *I Pagliacci.*

    4 *I play lightly . . . Dowland's languid song. Loth to depart:* Not a song title, but a generic name for a leave-taking song or tune. Joyce probably had in mind Dowland's "Now, O now, I needs must part." The allusion is vaguer in *A Portrait*, p. 219 (223), where Stephen is asked by the dark girl "to sing one of his curious songs. Then he saw himself sitting at the old piano, striking chords softly from its speckled keys and singing, amid the talk which had risen again in the room, to her who leaned beside the mantelpiece a dainty song of the Elizabethans, a sad and sweet loth to depart . . ."

      Here, opening from . . . and clip again: A Portrait, p. 233 (237).

10 1 *quia frigus erat:* "And the servants and officers stood there, who had made a fire of coals; for it was cold . . ." John 18:18.

      Upon the steps . . . ad Dominum: The prostration of the ministers, and the reading from Hosea 6:1–6, begin the Good Friday mass.

      She stands . . . sindark nave: Some of this imagery is used, with a different implication, in Joyce's poem "Nightpiece," dated "Trieste, 1915."

    2 *Perhaps, an . . . produce her image:* In discoursing on Shakespeare, Stephen declares, "The images of other males of his blood will repel him. He will see

in them grotesque attempts of nature to foretell or repeat himself." *Ulysses,* pp. 195–96 (250–51).

11	1	*Tie . . . simple knot:* Beatrice's death speech at the end of Shelley's *The Cenci.*

12   1   *A lady of letters:* "She lives in Leeson park, with a grief and kickshaws, a lady of letters." *Ulysses,* p. 48 (61).

12   3   *Loggione:* the top gallery in the opera house.

13   1   *My words . . . a quagmire:* The similar sentence in *A Portrait* is on p. 195 (199).

           4   *dark langour-flooded eyes:* Joyce corrects the spelling and takes over the phrase in *A Portrait,* p. 223 (227): "Her eyes, dark and with a look of languor, were opening to his eyes."

14   2   *Her eyes . . . abundant seed:* The same imaginary possession occurs in *A Portrait,* p. 223 (227):

"Her nakedness yielded to him, radiant, warm, odorous and lavishlimbed, enfolded him like a shining cloud, enfolded him like water with a liquid life: and like a cloud of vapour or like waters circumfluent in space the liquid letters of speech, symbols of the element of mystery, flowed forth over his brain."

Compare the dialogue in the last act of *Exiles,* p. 106 (144):

"ROBERT, *catching her hands:* Bertha! What happened last night? What is the truth that I am to tell? *He gazes earnestly into her eyes.* Were you mine in that sacred night of love? Or have I dreamed it?

BERTHA, *smiles faintly:* Remember your dream of me. You dreamed that I was yours last night.

ROBERT: And that is the truth—a dream? That is what I am to tell?

BERTHA: Yes.

Robert, *kisses both her hands:* Bertha! *In a softer voice.* In all my life only that dream is real. I forget the rest."

15   1   *Ralli's house:* Baron Ambrogio Ralli (1878–1938), a prominent Triestine, had a palazzo in Piazza Scorcola.

basilisk eyes . . . messer Brunetto: quoted from Brunetto Latini, *Il Tesoro,* translated by Bono Giamboni from Latini's French text, ed. P. Chabaille (Bologna, 1887, 4 vols.), II, pp. 137–38. Latini says of the basilisk that it poisons any man it sees. Compare "a jet of liquorish venom" in line 14 below.

In *Ulysses,* p. 194 (248–49), Joyce makes the Italian more colloquial:

"Stephen withstood the bane of miscreant eyes, glinting stern under wrinkled brows. A basilisk. *E quando vede l'uomo l'attosca.* Messer Brunetto, I thank thee for the word."

    3   *A soft . . . —Nora!—* Giacomo's dream calls up a scene later in time, when his pupil would be married and full of unexpectedly progressive sexual notions ("adultery of wisdom") as well as of infernal, serpentine designs upon him. Frightened by this fatal involvement, he wakes to reality and marital reassurance.

This dream contrasts with one Joyce reported later to Herbert Gorman, in which Molly Bloom—also posed later in time—tossed a coffinlike snuffbox at him, saying, "I have done with you, too, Mr. Joyce," while Ezra Pound (instead of Gogarty) stood by. Molly rejects him, while Giacomo's pupil is about to seduce him. As in one of his epiphanies, Joyce tremblingly longed for "an iniquitous abandonment," and made the possibility of it the scene of greatest tension in *Ulysses* as here.

16   1   *Jan Pieters Sweelink . . . an end:* Stephen talks with Bloom about this song in *Ulysses,* p. 663 (772–73):

"Exquisite variations he was now describing on an
air *Youth here has End* by Jans Pieter Sweelinck, a
Dutchman of Amsterdam where the frows come
from."

16   4   *a casque . . . blunt spear:* "Stephen looked down
on a wide headless caubeen, hung on his ashplant-
handle over his knee. My casque and sword."
Ulysses, p. 192 (246).

Ottocaro Weiss has been of the utmost help with the foregoing
notes, and thanks are given to him and to Walter Toscanini,
Stuart Small, Rev. J. C. Lehane, and Mabel Worthington.